For Matthew
~ CL

For Sven
~ GH

LITTLE TIGER PRESS
An imprint of Magi Publications
1 The Coda Centre, 189 Munster Road, London SW6 6AW
www.littletigerpress.com

First published in Great Britain 2003
by Little Tiger Press, London
This edition published 2008

Text copyright © Christine Leeson 2003
Illustrations copyright © Gaby Hansen 2003

ISBN 978-1-84506-812-7

Printed in China

1 3 5 7 9 10 8 6 4 2

MOLLY and the STORM

by Christine Leeson

Illustrated by Gaby Hansen

LITTLE TIGER PRESS

It was the first sunny day after weeks and
weeks of rain.
"Can we go out to play, Mom?" asked Molly
   Mouse, dancing in the pale sunshine. "Please?"
"As long as you keep an eye on the weather,"
   said Mother Mouse. "I'm sure more rain
   is on the way."

Molly and her brothers
and sister scampered across
the fields. They chased each other around
trees, puffy and white with blossoms.

They hopped through
carpets of bluebells.

They were enjoying themselves
so much that they didn't notice
it was suddenly getting darker.

Plop!
A large drop of rain fell on Molly's nose — then another and another. Big dark clouds filled the sky, and the rain started to fall faster and faster.
"We'll never get home in time," groaned Molly.
"Where can we find shelter until it stops?"

Just then, a squirrel hurried by on her way home. She <u>stopped</u> when she saw the wet little mice. Her own family was safe and warm in their nest. She couldn't possibly leave the mice out in the rain.

"Come with me," she said. "You can stay at my place."

Squirrel ran ahead and bounded
up a tree, but the mice didn't follow.
"Your house is too high and it doesn't
look safe in this storm," sighed Molly.

An old harvest mouse popped
her head out of the long grass.
"You can stay with me," she said kindly.
"I have a nice warm nest of twigs."

Harvest Mouse scuttled to her home, but the mice didn't follow. They could see that her woven nest was far too small for all of them.

Just then a little rabbit found the mice. "You can come to my place," cried Rabbit, "and join my baby brothers and sisters in the warmth of our burrow." He couldn't leave these poor little mice out in the storm.

for

fell

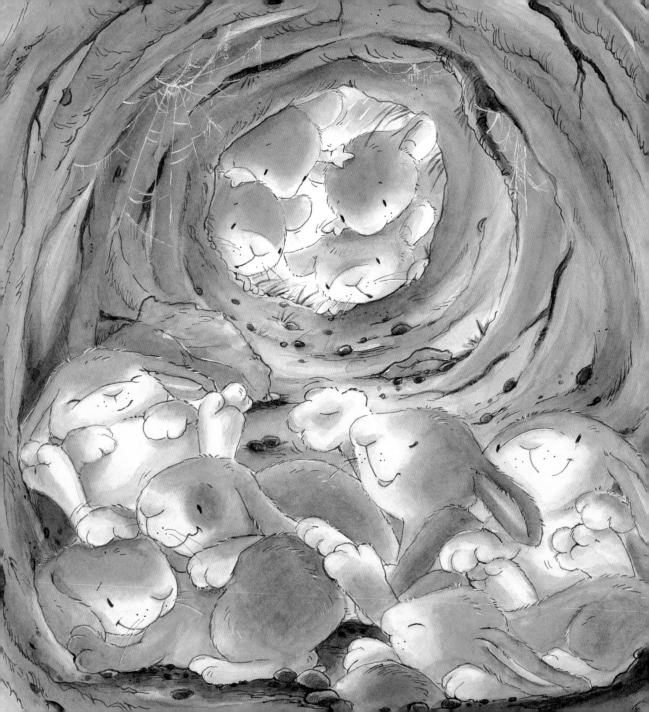

Rabbit hopped down his rabbit hole, but the
mice stayed outside. "Your home is very full,"
said Molly, peering inside at all the baby rabbits.
"I think we'd be too squished."

Before Rabbit had time to answer, he and the mice
heard someone calling. Molly pricked up her ears.
"It's Mom!" she squeaked.

"Thank goodness I've found you!"
cried Mother Mouse. "The storm
is getting worse. But there's
an old hollow oak tree nearby
where we can stay dry until
the rain stops."

The hollow oak tree stood at the top of
a slope. The mice scrambled inside and
were soon warm and dry.
"We'll stay here tonight," said Mother
Mouse. "You can all curl up together
and go to sleep."

But Molly couldn't sleep. She lay listening
to the roar of the wind and the pounding rain,
and she was worried about her new friends.
Would Harvest Mouse's home be destroyed?
Rabbit's burrow might be flooded, and
Squirrel's nest blown away.

Molly looked at her family, sleeping snugly.
She couldn't leave her friends out in the storm.
Molly hurried outside.

The wind tugged and pulled at Molly as she struggled across the field. There, huddled under a swaying tree, was Squirrel.

"You must come with me," said Molly. "We've found the perfect place to stay."

Just then, Harvest Mouse appeared out of
the grass, looking tired and messy.
"Can I come too?" she asked.
"Of course," said Molly.

As they made their way back,
they passed Rabbit and
his family huddled
under a bush. "You'll
be nice and warm if
you come with us,"
said Molly.

At last Molly and her new friends reached the shelter of the old oak tree. Outside, the wind battered the trees and flattened the grass. But inside, everyone was safe and dry.

The wind had stopped by the time morning came,
and as the sun crept up into the sky the animals
crawled out of their shelter. There before them was
a rainbow, stretching as far as the eye could see.

"It's for you, Molly," whispered Harvest Mouse.
"It's a special present for saving us."
    And Molly smiled happily, surrounded by her
family and all her new friends.